My Snuggle Up Bedtime Treasury

This igloo book belongs to:

....

igloobooks

Published in 2019
by Igloo Books Ltd
Cottage Farm
Sywell
NN6 0BJ
www.igloobooks.com

0919 001.01
2 4 6 8 10 9 7 5 3 1
ISBN 978-1-78905-486-6

Written by Kathryn Beer, Hannah Campling,
Hannah Cather, Stephanie Moss and Caroline Richards
Illustrated by Gareth Llewhellin
Additional illustration by Tom Heard

Designed by Jason Shortland
Edited by Hannah Cather

Printed and manufactured in China

Contents

igloobooks

Bedtime Races

Millie and Max were the most competitive brother and sister ever. No matter what they were doing, each one was always desperate to beat the other. One evening, they were both so busy trying to win a game of snap that they refused to go to bed when Mum asked.

"Not yet, Mum, I'm about to wiiiin!" cried Millie.
"No, I am!" called Max. Mum had had enough,
so she decided to come up with a game of her own.

"I've got a better idea," she said.
"Who can be the first one to run to your bedroom?"

5

Millie and Max stopped what they
were doing and looked at each other.
Then they jumped up and ran towards
their room as fast as they could.
"Me first!" cried Max.

"No, ME first!" called Millie, chasing behind him.
Finally, Mum declared Max the winner.

"Again!" cried Millie. "I can beat him."
"Okay," said Mum. "Who can put on their pyjamas first?"

So they raced off again to find some pyjamas. This time Millie came first, leaving Max with his head stuck in his top!

By now, Millie and Max had each won a round in Mum's game.
They were having so much fun, they wanted to keep playing.

So Mum challenged them to be
the first to tidy away their toys...

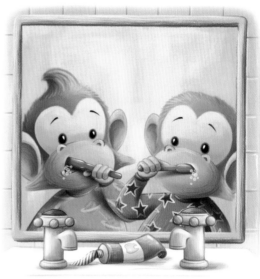

... the first to brush their teeth...

... and the first to get under the bedcovers.

"Maybe there's just time for one more round," said Mum, grinning.
"To win the game, who can be the first to close their eyes and....?"
Before Mum could finish, Millie and Max had already fallen asleep.
They would have to settle for a draw in this game tonight!

Somewhere to Sleep

It was a warm summer night on Peanut Lane. Everywhere was quiet, except for one very noisy house. Grace the elephant had a baby brother and he was keeping everyone awake. It didn't matter what they did, Baby Ollie just wasn't ready to go to bed.

Grace tried her best to sleep, but there was just too much noise.
So, she climbed out of bed and went to the nursery to help.

She reached into Baby Ollie's cot and gave him his rattle,
but he threw it on the floor and cried even louder!

Grace tried to get her mum's attention. "Mum, it's too loud!"
she shouted, covering her ears. "I can't sleep!" But poor Mum and
Dad were so tired, and Baby Ollie was making so much noise,
that they couldn't hear her over all of his crying.

Back in bed, Grace put a pillow over her ears. Then, she had a bright idea. "If I can't get to sleep here," she thought, "I'll just have to find somewhere else to sleep."

So, she picked up her favourite teddy bear and cosiest blanket and plodded down the stairs.

First, Grace made a den between the kitchen table and the sink,
but the tap was leaking and made a loud DRIP-DRIP-DRIP.
"This is still too noisy," she sighed.

Looking around, she spotted
her toy box. She tried to squeeze
inside but she couldn't quite fit.
"I know," said Grace,
"I'll try the armchair."

Grace climbed onto the lumpy chair, but it wasn't very comfortable. As she rolled over, Grace felt something hard. Feeling underneath the cushion, she found her toy whale!

"I don't think I'll ever find somewhere to sleep, and I'm just so t-t-tired," she said, with a big yawn.

Suddenly, Grace noticed the crying had stopped. She tiptoed to the bottom of the stairs and listened. Instead, she could hear a low rumbling sound. "What now?" she grumbled. "I'll go and see."

First, she looked in the nursery and then she checked
the bathroom, but Grace couldn't find the new noise.

She also couldn't find Mum,
Dad or Baby Ollie anywhere!
"Where could they be?"
wondered Grace.

Peeping into the last room, Grace found everyone fast asleep. The noise was Dad's snoring! "This might not be the perfect place to sleep, but I'm so tired I think it'll do," said Grace. Mum opened her sleepy eyes and lifted her up for a cuddle.

Grace squeezed in between Mum and Dad and snuggled under
the covers. Baby Ollie gurgled and wrapped his trunk around Grace's.
They all cuddled in close and soon drifted off to sleep. Goodnight!

Can't-decide Connie

Connie couldn't make a decision. Whenever she tried, her answer was the same. "I can't decide!" At bedtime, it was worse. The spotty or starry pyjamas? Should the windows be open or closed?

Night lights, on or off? Which teddy to cuddle?
Which bedtime story? There were too many choices!

It was the same each night and Mum knew she
had to do something. She tried one last time.
"Connie, would you like some milk or water?"
Connie blinked. "I... um... I... I can't decide!"

"Okay," said Mum. "Why don't you
try not making any decisions
at all? Let's see what happens!"

So, Connie put both pairs of pyjamas on, and drank the milk and water one after the other.

She turned one light on and one off, opened one window and closed the other.

She even squeezed into bed with both of her favourite teddies, until there was no room left at all!

Finally, Mum read one bedtime story and was just about
to read the second, when Connie jumped up and cried, "STOP!"
She was too full, too hot, too uncomfortable and much
too tired to listen to another story.

When Mum got up and turned off the light,
Connie knew she had to change.

23

The next morning, Connie knew exactly what to do. "I'll be a Can-decide Connie today!" she told herself and ran down to the kitchen.

"What would you like for breakfast, Connie?" asked Dad. To his surprise, Connie didn't hesitate. "Toast and jam, please!"

Later, in the garden,
Connie's brother asked,
"What should we play?"
Connie didn't think
for long. "Catch!"

Even Ronnie the dog got
the Can-decide-Connie
treatment. "Let's go to
the park for your walk.
Come on, Dad!"

25

After a day full of decision-making, it was soon bedtime. Mum returned from work to find that Connie had already chosen which pyjamas to wear, which bedtime book to read and which teddy to snuggle.

"You're making so many decisions, Connie!"
said Mum, happily. Bedtime had never been so easy.

Connie felt tired after her busy day, so Mum soon tucked her into bed and kissed her goodnight. Just before leaving, Mum asked, "Shall I leave the door open or closed?"

"Um... well... I... I can't..." Connie paused, smiling.
"I'm joking! Closed, please, Mummy!"

Big Bed

After bath time and a story, it was time for bed.
Mum tucked in Tommy, with his toy fire engine, Fred.
But Tommy cried, "This bed's so small, and it's lumpy, too.
I need something bigger, better and... totally brand new!"

The next day Tommy heard a CLATTER,
a WHIRR, a BANG and a BASH.
"What's going on?" he thought,
when he heard something go CRASH!

What Tommy didn't know was that Mum had planned a surprise.
And Dad had secretly helped her gather tools and supplies.

Mum worked hard all week, until the big bedtime reveal.
She'd built a fire-engine bed, with a great big steering wheel!

As he climbed up the ladder, Tommy cried, "This is the best bed ever!"

Then, he quietly fell asleep for the first night in forever.

33

Hattie's Castle

Hattie Hedgehog had spent all morning making a castle from cardboard boxes. It was so special that she didn't want to share it with anyone else. After lunch, Dad knocked on the castle door. "Your cousins are here for a sleepover!" he called.

Ella and Jack rushed into the room.
"Can we play with you, Hattie?"
asked Jack, running towards her.
"I want to be a knight!" cried Ella.
But Hattie wouldn't let them join in.
It was her castle!

35

At first, Hattie loved having the castle all to herself.
She pretended to be a princess and had a feast in the Great Hall,
with tasty jelly, cupcakes and jam sandwiches.

She even bravely scared away an imaginary dragon with her sword.

But after a while, Hattie felt bored. It wasn't much fun having a feast on her own and no one cheered when she defeated the dragon. Hattie sat in the tower and looked sadly out of the window.

She noticed that her cousins were giggling, surrounded by paints and card. "They're having much more fun!" she said and went over to them. "I'm sorry I didn't share my castle with you." Ella smiled. "That's okay. Look at what we've done!"

Ella had made an awesome knight's shield, and Jack had made
a scary green dragon mask. "Wow!" said Hattie. "They're fantastic!"
She showed her cousins around the castle and they decorated it.
Soon, it was even more amazing, with flags and a drawbridge.

At bedtime, the little hedgehogs didn't want to stop playing, so Dad came up with an idea to help. Princess Hattie was just rescuing the knight from the scary dragon, when Dad returned with sleeping bags. "A castle sleepover!" gasped Hattie.

Once they'd finished a bedtime snack, the cousins snuggled
into their sleeping bags. Hattie thought the castle looked magical
when they shone their torches through the window. Everyone soon
fell straight to sleep, dreaming of castle adventures.

Ben's Dreamland

Ben didn't like bedtime at all. It was boring!
If he had his own way, he'd stay up all night
reading books, making up stories for his toys
and thinking up all kinds of magical worlds.

So, Ben's dad came up with an idea to help.
He told him about a place where fun things always happened.
"It's called Dreamland!" said Dad. "To get there, just close your eyes."
Ben couldn't wait, so he closed his eyes and fell fast asleep.

Whoosh! Suddenly, Ben was soaring through space!
He was on a shooting star, flying through the sparkly sky.
"Careful!" shouted Arty Astronaut. Then Ben saw some
aliens, who waved and wiggled their tentacles!

Before long, Ben had slid along the ring of a planet, eaten a picnic of mooncakes and gobbled up stardust sandwiches. "If you think this is fun, see what's down there!" Arty said, pointing to an enormous black hole. "Dive right in!"

45

Splash! Ben dived underwater and a group of splish-sploshing fish swam by him. It was then that he spotted some gold glinting on the seabed. Hidden treasure! He was just about to pick up one of the coins when… "Arrrr!" came a distant cry.

Ben saw a swashbuckling pirate heading towards him!
"That's Captain Purplebeard! He wants his treasure back!"
said Marigold Mermicorn, her tail swishing in the water.
"Quick, hide in the cave over there! Hurry!"

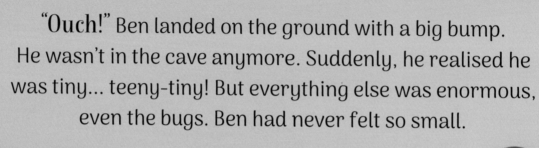

"Ouch!" Ben landed on the ground with a big bump. He wasn't in the cave anymore. Suddenly, he realised he was tiny... teeny-tiny! But everything else was enormous, even the bugs. Ben had never felt so small.

"Ben!" called Babs Butterfly, but Ben didn't hear her. He'd just spotted a huge spider lurking in the shadows, watching and waiting! "Don't worry!" shouted Babs. "Hop onto my wings. I'll help you!" They flew up into the sky.

"Wow!" Up in the sky, Ben landed on a soft, fluffy cloud.
Boing! He bounced up and down, surrounded by cupcakes and
colourful sweets. "Hello, Ben!" called Poppy the pony as she
bounced her way over to him. "Are you hungry?"

50

Poppy nibbled the cloud. "This tastes of marshmallow!"
she cried, before dipping a hoof in a rainbow and licking it.
"All these sweets are delicious. Try one!" she said.
Ben was just reaching for a candy cane when...

51

... Brrring! Ben opened his eyes. It was his alarm clock. He yawned and stretched, then thought about all his magical adventures with Arty, Marigold and Poppy. Dreamland was amazing! He had to get back there.

So, Ben closed his eyes
and snuggled down in bed.
Then, he noticed something small
and round under his pillow.

He pulled it out slowly... it was
one of Captain Purplebeard's coins!
"Wow!" said Ben. "It wasn't just
a dream. I can't wait for bedtime
to have another adventure!"

53

Do You Believe in Fairies?

Bunny loved her fairy wings and swishing her wand in the air,
but she wondered why she'd never seen a fairy anywhere.

"I wish I could meet a fairy," said Bunny, shutting her eyes tight.

But her wish didn't come true.
There were no fairies in sight!

"Do YOU believe in fairies?" Bunny asked Mummy one day.
"Of course I do," said Mummy, leading her outside to play.

"There are fairies all around," she said, "but they're hard to see.
Sometimes they leave clues to find, so come and look with me!"

They found a fairy ring of toadstools, of purple, pink and red.
"This is where the fairies dance around together," Mummy said.

Fairy
Dust

There was a hidden box of fairy dust by the garden pond
and a fairy house appeared when Bunny waved her magic wand.

"Let's have a fairy tea party," said Mummy. "Look... surprise!"
Then, as the sun was shining, they saw rain fall from the skies.

A rainbow soon appeared and Bunny squealed with delight.
"So magic's real, after all. See, Mummy, you were right!"

Bath-time Pirate

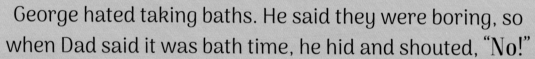

George hated taking baths. He said they were boring, so when Dad said it was bath time, he hid and shouted, "No!"

Dad quickly made a plan
so that George would take a dip.
He would turn their normal bath
into an awesome pirate ship!

Dad made a ship's wheel and turned the curtain into sails.
He even found a telescope so George could look for whales!

When George saw his ship, he jumped in with a SPLASH!
"Yo-ho-ho!" he cried. "Look at my treasure stash!"

65

George splashed for hours and played pirates with his dad.
"I told you, George!" he said. "Baths really aren't so bad."

From then on, George changed his mind. Who would have guessed?
Now the giraffe who hated baths thought they were the best!

The Croc Who Can

It was Colin Crocodile's fifth birthday and he felt very grown up. "Let's find you something to wear for your party," said Mum. But Colin shook his head. "I can do it all by myself," he said and raced upstairs.

Colin spotted the dressing-up box and had an idea.
"**I'm ready!**" he shouted, zooming downstairs a little bit later.
His sister, Cara, giggled when she saw him wearing his pirate
T-shirt, superhero cape, fairy wings and space helmet.

In the kitchen, Dad was making the party food.
"Can I help?" asked Colin, washing his hands and
putting an apron on over his special party outfit.

"Yes, please," said Dad, "you can finish the sandwiches."
Suddenly, the phone rang and Dad went to answer it.
"These sandwiches are boring," thought Colin.

Instead, he searched for all his favourite things to eat.
He mixed together chocolate, ice cream, crisps and pineapple.

"Try this!" said Colin, when
Dad came back into the kitchen.
Dad took a very tiny bite.
"Yum!" he said, but Colin was sure
he saw Dad pull a funny face.

So, Colin went to help with the decorations instead.
He wanted to put up the banner without any help from Mum,
but as he raced past the balloons, they burst with a loud POP!
"I can't do anything properly," said Colin, starting to cry.

Mum gave Colin a big hug. "Don't be silly," she said, "you can do lots of things really well!" She reminded Colin how he had made Cara laugh with his superhero-pirate-fairy costume, and how kind he had been to offer to make the sandwiches.

73

"Everyone makes mistakes," explained Mum.
"To get better, you just have to try again!" Then, she took
Colin to the kitchen where there was an enormous cake.
"You can decorate it all by yourself," she said.

When everyone arrived for the party, Colin's amazing
cake was covered in colourful icing, sprinkles and sweets.
Mum put candles on top and everyone sang Happy Birthday.
"Well done, Colin," they said. "The croc who can!"

Double Trouble

Katie and Lizzie were identical twins. If it wasn't for their different clothes and glasses, it would be impossible to tell them apart! They had the same orange fur and the same little pink noses. However, everything they did was the opposite.

When Katie played outside,
Lizzie stayed inside.

If Katie said, "Yes!",
Lizzie said, "No!"

When Lizzie wore spots,
Katie wore stripes.

If Lizzie had a hot chocolate,
Katie wanted a cold drink.

They were very different indeed!

Poor Dad always had to come up with different activities!
So, he made a new suggestion. "Let's all watch a film!"
he said, but the twins wanted different films, snacks
and drinks. Dad slumped on the sofa with a sigh.

The twins looked at each other in surprise.
They hadn't meant to cause any trouble. "I've got an idea!"
said Katie. "Tomorrow, let's try and do the same things."
Lizzie agreed. "That will be much easier for Dad!"

The next day, the twins started their plan. In the morning, they both wanted the same dungarees, but there was only one pair!

Without deciding what to do, they went to eat some breakfast. **"Porridge for us both!"** Lizzie said, but there wasn't enough.

Afterwards, the girls headed to their toy box. They tried to play with the same teddy, but it ended up in a teddy tug-of-war!

Instead, they went to play on the slide. But when they tried to go down together, they got stuck!

At bedtime, the twins wanted the same dressing gown,
and when Dad read a story, they both tried to turn the pages.
Then, when they started to give Dad a cuddle and ended up a
bundle of tangled paws, they had all had enough.

"It's hard being exactly the same!" the twins moaned.
Dad quickly realised what they had been up to and laughed.
"You don't need to change at all!" he said. "You might be opposite
little kittens, but I love you just the way you are!"

The Northern Lights

Polly the polar bear had started to feel afraid at bedtime. So, every night, she would make a new excuse to stay up as long as she could. She'd always want one more story, one more kiss on the forehead or one more mug of hot chocolate.

One evening, Polly was on her third story. "It's bedtime now,"
said Mum, but Polly started to cry. "There's a monster in my room!"
she cried. "That's why I don't want to sleep." Mum gave her a big
cuddle and said, "Oh, Polly, there's no such thing as monsters!"

Mum checked under Polly's bed and
in the wardrobe, before tucking Polly in.
"Night, night," she whispered, closing the door.
Suddenly, Polly's room became dark. She could
see shadows on the floor and felt very scared.

Polly pulled the covers up to
her nose and cuddled Teddy close.
All of a sudden, something big and
green shone through her window.
It glowed brightly and moved
without a sound. Polly gulped.
It was the monster!

The monster began to creep into her room, getting closer
and closer. "Muuuum!" shouted Polly, as loud as she could.
"Come quick! The big green monster is back!"

Mum ran into Polly's room and looked to where she was pointing.
"There, on the wall!" squeaked Polly, as she ducked under the covers.
Mum smiled. "That's not a monster," she said, gently.

"I'm going to take you on a special journey to show you there's nothing to be scared of. Put on your dressing gown and come with me," said Mum, holding out her hand.

Together, they left their igloo and went outside, down the frosty garden path and into the snow.

As they crunched down the lane, Polly heard the sound of friendly voices. It was Norman Narwhal and Percy Penguin. "Have you come to watch, too?" they asked. Polly was puzzled, but Mum just smiled and carried on walking.

As they passed a hole
in the ice, an excited walrus
jumped up. "Hello! I'm sure
you can't wait to see!" he said.
Polly was very confused.
"Where are we going, Mum?"
"You'll find out," replied Mum,
with a small smile.

Soon afterwards, they turned a corner and Polly saw a crowd of animals. "Hello!" they all said. They looked as though they were waiting for something. "I wonder what this has to do with the green monster from my bedroom?" Polly wondered.

Suddenly, Mum pointed upwards and whispered, "Look!"
To Polly's surprise, the sky was filled with beautiful coloured lights.
"There's your monster!" said Mum. The lights danced and rippled
across the sky. Polly gasped. "It's amazing!" she replied.

"We live in a very special part of the world, where sometimes
we get to see these shimmering lights in the sky," explained Mum.
"We come every single year!" said Norman and Percy, happily.
Polly watched the lights until it was time to go home.

Back in their igloo, Polly snuggled into bed.
"How about a hot drink or a story?" asked Mum,
but Polly didn't need either. She wasn't afraid
any more and had already fallen asleep!